Mousekin's Special Day

A book about special days

BY JANE BELK MONCURE • ILLUSTRATED BY MERNIE GALLAGHER-COLE

The Child's World

Published by The Child's World®
1980 Lookout Drive • Mankato, MN 56003-1705
800-599-READ • www.childsworld.com

Acknowledgments
The Child's World®: Mary Berendes, Publishing Director
The Design Lab: Design
Jody Jensen Shaffer: Editing

ISBN 9781623235864
LCCN 2013931389

Printed in the United States of America
Mankato, MN
July 2013
PA02177

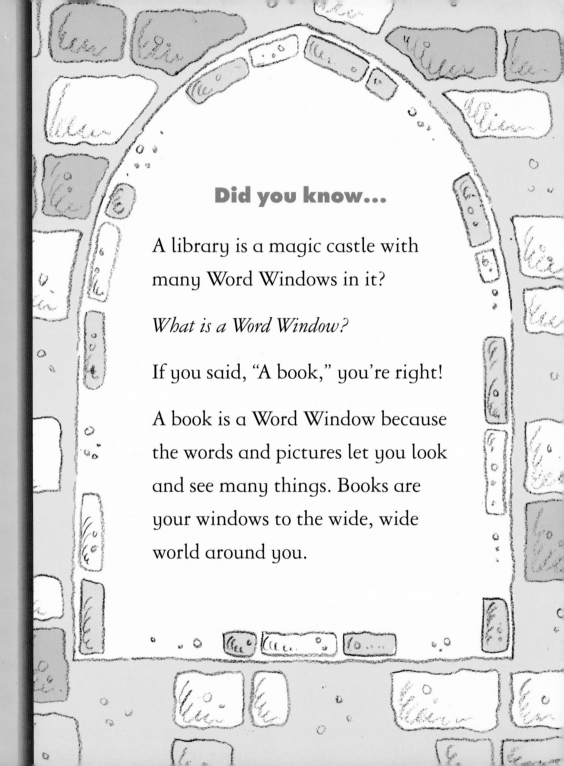

Did you know...

A library is a magic castle with many Word Windows in it?

What is a Word Window?

If you said, "A book," you're right!

A book is a Word Window because the words and pictures let you look and see many things. Books are your windows to the wide, wide world around you.

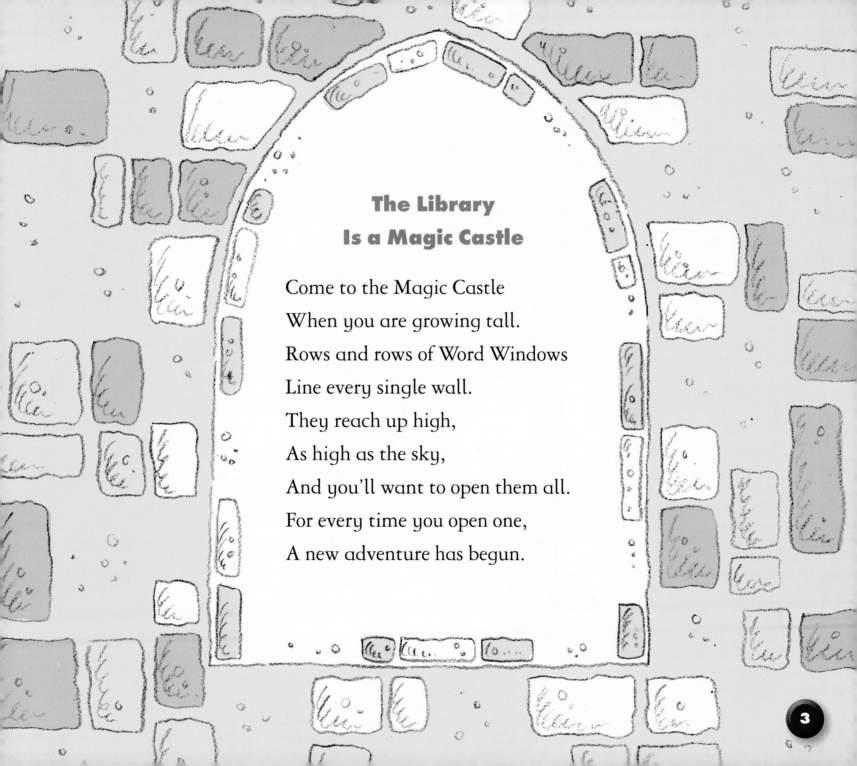

The Library
Is a Magic Castle

Come to the Magic Castle
When you are growing tall.
Rows and rows of Word Windows
Line every single wall.
They reach up high,
As high as the sky,
And you'll want to open them all.
For every time you open one,
A new adventure has begun.

Ted opened a Word Window.
Here is what he read:

"Wake up, Mousekin," said Mama Mouse.
"Today is a special day."

"What special day?" asked Mousekin.
"You know," said Mama.

"Is today Valentine's Day?" asked Mousekin.
She smiled a big smile.

"No," said Mama. "Today is not Valentine's Day.
We have no valentines in this house today."

"Is today Easter day?" asked Mousekin.
"No," said Mama. "We have no Easter baskets
  in this house today."

"Is today the Fourth of July?" said Mousekin.
She played her drum. Tum, tum, tum.

"No," said Mama. "Today is not the Fourth of July. We have no flags in this house today."

"What are you making?" asked Mousekin.
"A surprise," said Mama. "Now run outside
and play."

Mousekin played with her ball.
"This ball looks like a pumpkin.
It makes me think of another special day."

Mousekin ran into the house.
"Is today Halloween?" she asked.

"No," said Mama. "You know today is not Halloween. We have no pumpkins in this house today."

"Hmmm," said Mousekin. "Today is not
Valentine's Day, nor Easter, nor the Fourth of
July, nor Halloween."

"Maybe today is Thanksgiving Day.
Maybe we will have a Thanksgiving party."

"We will have a party, but not a Thanksgiving party," said Mama. "Guess again."

"I cannot think of another special day,"
said Mousekin.
"Yes you can," said Mama.

Just then, Papa Mouse came home
with a gift.

"Hooray!" said Mousekin.
"Today must be Christmas!"

"No," said Papa. "Today is not Christmas."

Then Mama put a big cake on the table.

"Now I know," said Mousekin, jumping up and down. "Today is someone's birthday."

"Yes," said Mama. "It is the birthday of someone very special."

"Is today your birthday, Mama?"
Mama shook her head no.

"Is today your birthday, Papa?"
Papa shook his head no.

"Then today must be *my* birthday,"
said Mousekin. "This is my own special day.
I knew it all along!"

"Happy birthday, Mousekin!" said her friends.

"A happy birthday is the very best special day
of all," Mousekin said.

Ted closed the Word Window.

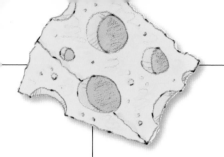

Questions and Activities

(Write your answers on a sheet of paper.)

1. Where does this story happen?
    Name two important things about that place.

2. Name two things you learned about special days.
    What else would you like to know?

3. Did this story have any words you don't know?
    How can you find out what they mean?

4. What does Mousekin's ball remind her of?
    What special day does this make her think of?

5. Tell this story to a friend. Take only two minutes.
    Which parts did you share?

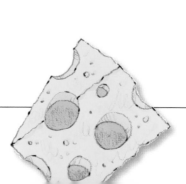